D0209240

JON SCIESZKA'S TRUCKTOWN

DIZZY IZZY

WRITTEN BY JON SCIESZKA

CHARACTERS ANXD ENVIRONMENTS DEVELOPED BY THE

DAVID SHANNON   **LOREN LONG**   **DAVID GORDON**

ILLUSTRATION CREW:

Executive producer: TOT INDUSTRIES in association with Animagic S.L.
Creative supervisor: Nina Rappaport Brown ○ Drawings by: Dan Root ○ Color by: Christopher Oatley
Art director: Karin Paprocki

Ready-to-Read

Simon Spotlight
New York   London   Toronto   Sydney   New Delhi

SIMON SPOTLIGHT

An imprint of Simon & Schuster Children's Publishing Division

1230 Avenue of the Americas, New York, New York 10020

Text and illustrations copyright © 2010 by JRS Worldwide, LLC.

SIMON SPOTLIGHT, READY-TO-READ, and colophon

are registered trademarks of Simon & Schuster, Inc.

TRUCKTOWN and JON SCIESZKA'S TRUCKTOWN and design

are trademarks of JRS Worldwide, LLC.

For information about special discounts for bulk purchases,

please contact Simon & Schuster Special Sales at 1-866-506-1949 or business@simonandschuster.com.

The Simon & Schuster Speakers Bureau can bring authors to your live event.

For more information or to book an event contact the Simon & Schuster Speakers Bureau

at 1-866-248-3049 or visit our website at www.simonspeakers.com.

The text of this book was set in Truck King. / Manufactured in the United States of America

0814 LAK / First Simon Spotlight hardcover edition / 10 9 8 7 6 5

Library of Congress Cataloging-in-Publication Data / Scieszka, Jon.

Dizzy Izzy / by Jon Scieszka ; artwork by the Design Garage: David Gordon,

Loren Long, David Shannon. / p. cm.–(Trucktown. Ready-to-roll.)

Summary: Izzy the ice cream truck tries to get himself dizzy.

[1. Ice cream trucks–Fiction. 2. Trucks–Fiction.] I. Design Garage. II. Title. / PZ7.S41267Diz 2010

[E]—dc22 / 2008024360

ISBN 978-1-4814-1460-9 (hc) / ISBN 978-1-4169-4145-3 (pbk) / ISBN 978-1-4814-1078-6 (eBook)

This is Izzy.

Izzy loves to get **dizzy.**

But is he?

Izzy gets
busy.

But Izzy is not dizzy.

Is he?

Izzy skids in a tizzy.
But Izzy is not dizzy.

Is he?

Izzy gets fizzy.
But Izzy is not dizzy.

Is he?

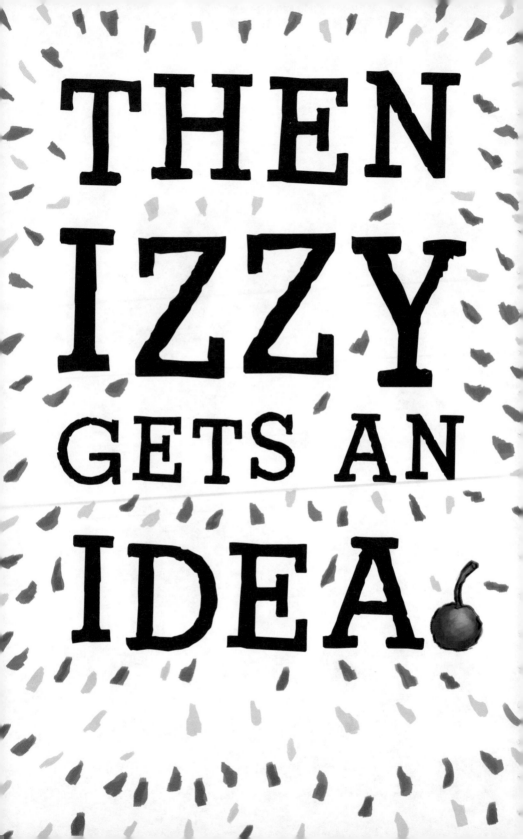

THEN IZZY GETS AN IDEA.

"Do you want an ice cream?
Do you want an ice cream?
Do you want an ice cream?"

Izzy whizzes.

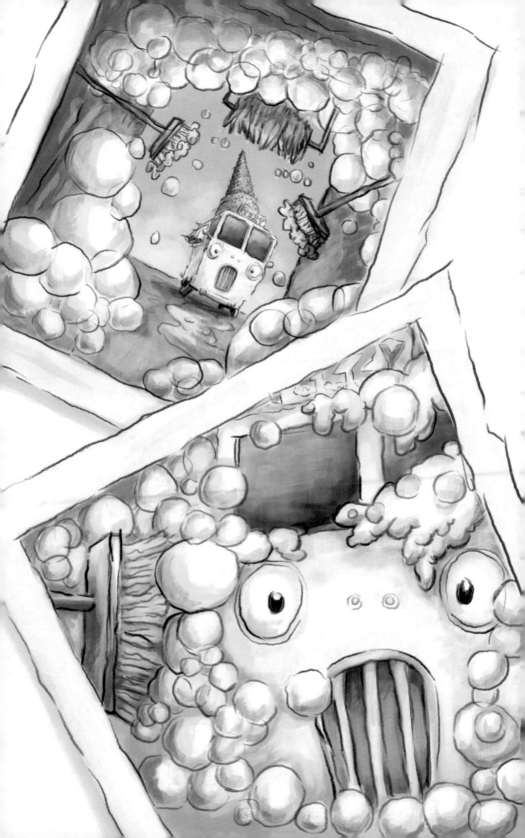

Izzy fizzes.

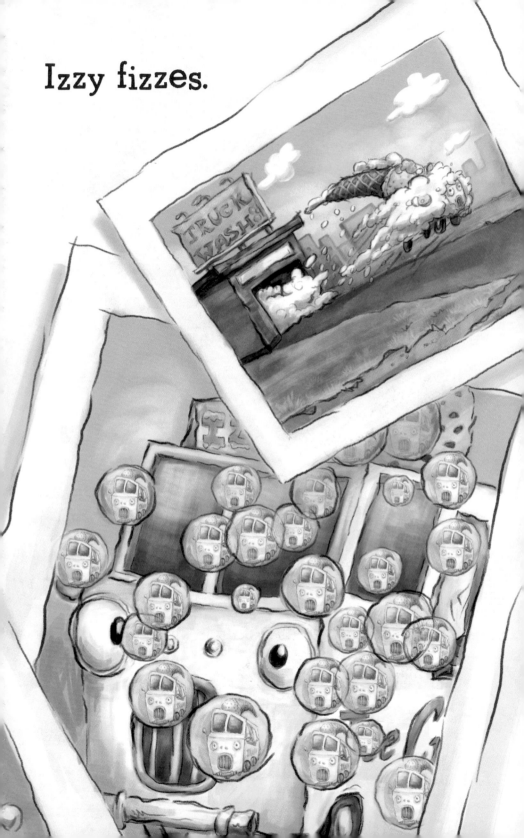

Izzy gets busy and fizzy
and all whizzy
in a tizzy.

Izzy is
dizzy!

But
guess
what?

Now Izzy thinks
he was fuzzy.

Was he?